ABOUT TUTTLE
"Books to Span the East and West"

Our core mission at Tuttle Publishing is to create books which bring people together one page at a time. Tuttle was founded in 1832 in the small New England town of Rutland, Vermont (USA). Our fundamental values remain as strong today as they were then—to publish best-in-class books informing the English-speaking world about the countries and peoples of Asia. The world has become a smaller place today and Asia's economic, cultural and political influence has expanded, yet the need for meaningful dialogue and information about this diverse region has never been greater. Since 1948, Tuttle has been a leader in publishing books on the cultures, arts, cuisines, languages and literatures of Asia. Our authors and photographers have won numerous awards and Tuttle has published thousands of books on subjects ranging from martial arts to paper crafts. We welcome you to explore the wealth of information available on Asia at **www.tuttlepublishing.com**.

Published by Tuttle Publishing, an imprint of Periplus Editions (HK) Ltd.

www.tuttlepublishing.com

Copyright © 2008 Periplus Editions (HK) Ltd.

Library of Congress Cataloging-in-Publication Data

Sakade, Florence.
  Peach Boy and other Japanese children's favorite stories / compiled by Florence Sakade; illustrated by Yoshisuke Kurosaki. — 1st ed.
     49 p. : col. ill. ; 24 cm.
  Summary: A collection of traditional Japanese folktales, including "Peach Boy," "The Magic Teakettle," and "The Tongue-Cut Sparrow."
  ISBN 978-4-8053-0996-4 (hardcover : alk. paper)
1. Tales—Japan. [1. Folklore—Japan.] I. Kurosaki, Yoshisuke, 1905– ill.
II. Title.
  PZ8.1.S2155Pe 2008
  [398.20952]—dc22
                                    2007052483

ISBN 978-4-8053-0996-4

Distributed by:

North America, Latin America & Europe
Tuttle Publishing
364 Innovation Drive,
North Clarendon, VT 05759-9436 U.S.A.
Tel: 1 (802) 773-8930; Fax: 1 (802) 773-6993
info@tuttlepublishing.com
www.tuttlepublishing.com

Japan
Tuttle Publishing
Yaekari Building, 3rd Floor
5-4-12 Osaki, Shinagawa-ku, Tokyo 141 0032
Tel: (81) 3 5437-0171; Fax: (81) 3 5437-0755
sales@tuttle.co.jp
www.tuttle.co.jp

Asia Pacific
Berkeley Books Pte. Ltd.
61 Tai Seng Avenue #02-12
Singapore 534167
Tel: (65) 6280-1330; Fax: (65) 6280-6290
inquiries@periplus.com.sg
www.periplus.com

First edition
19 18 17 16   10 9 8 7 6 5 4   1603RR

Printed in China

Peach Boy

And Other Japanese Children's Favorite Stories

Compiled by Florence Sakade

Illustrated by Yoshisuke Kurosaki

TUTTLE Publishing

Tokyo | Rutland, Vermont | Singapore

Contents

Publisher's Foreword

In today's ever-shrinking world—where e-mails zoom from one continent to another in the space of a heartbeat, where travelers can easily pass through political boundaries once more solid than stone—understanding and tolerance have never been at a higher premium. Parents and teachers are increasingly aware of the need for children to be citizens of this small world who will grow into thinking adults who, while proud of their own traditions and heritage, respect the varied experiences and viewpoints to be found in other cultures.

This collection of traditional stories can help set children on this enlightened path, introducing them to marvelous characters and places that have been loved by Japanese children for centuries.

Each of these stories—amusing, instructive and wise—is to be found in many forms and versions in Japan, and often in other countries as well. We have tried to select the most interesting version in each case and, in our translations, to remain true to the spirit of the Japanese originals. At the same time we have explained in the stories customs and situations that Western readers might not understand.

These timeless stories have both united and delighted children for hundreds of years, and will continue to do so for countless generations to come.

Peach Boy

Once upon a time there lived in Japan a kind old man and his wife. The old man was a woodcutter. He and his wife were very sad and lonely because they had no children.

One day the old man went into the mountains to cut firewood, and the old woman went to the river to wash clothes.

No sooner had the old woman begun her washing than she was very surprised to see a big peach floating down the river. It was the biggest peach she'd ever seen in all her life. She pulled the peach out of the river and decided to take it home and share it with the old man for their supper that night.

Late in the afternoon the old man came home, and the old woman said to him, "Look what a wonderful peach I've found for our supper." The old man said it was truly a beautiful peach. He was very hungry and said, "Let's divide it and eat it right away."

So the old woman brought a big knife from the kitchen and got ready to cut the peach in half. But just then a human voice called out from inside the peach. "Wait! Don't cut me!" cried the voice. Suddenly the peach split open, and a beautiful baby boy jumped out of the peach.

The old man and woman were astounded. But the baby said, "Don't be afraid. The God of Heaven saw how lonely you were without any children, so he sent me to be your son."

The old man and woman were very happy, and they took the baby to be their son. Since he was born from a peach, they named him Momotaro, which means Peach Boy. They loved Momotaro very much and raised him to be a fine boy.

When Momotaro was fifteen years old, he said to his mother and father, "You have always been very kind to me. Now I am grown and I must do something to help our land. In a distant part of the sea is an island named Ogre Island. Many wicked ogres live there, and they often come here and do bad things like carrying people away and stealing our things. So I'm going to go to Ogre Island to fight them and bring back the treasures that they've stolen. Please let me do this!"

Momotaro's mother and father were surprised to hear this, but they were also very proud of Momotaro for wanting to help other people. So they helped Momotaro get ready for his journey to Ogre Island. The old man gave him a sword and some armor, and the old woman fixed him a good lunch of millet dumplings. Then Momotaro began his journey, promising his parents that he would be home soon.

Momotaro went walking toward the sea. It was a long way. As he went along, he met a brown dog. The dog growled at Momotaro and was about to bite him, but then Momotaro gave him one of his dumplings. He told the dog that he was going to fight the ogres on Ogre Island. So the brown dog said he would go along, too, to help Momotaro.

Momotaro and the brown dog kept on walking and soon they met a monkey. The dog and the monkey started to have a fight. But Momotaro told the monkey that they were going to fight the ogres on Ogre Island. Then the monkey asked if he could go with them. So Momotaro gave the monkey a dumpling and let him join them.

Momotaro, the brown dog and the monkey kept on walking and soon they met a pheasant. The dog, the monkey and the pheasant were about to start fighting when Momotaro told the pheasant they were going to fight the ogres on Ogre Island. The pheasant asked if he could go too. So Momotaro gave the pheasant a dumpling and told him to come along with them.

So, with Momotaro as their general, the brown dog, the monkey and the pheasant, who usually hated each other, became good and faithful friends. They walked a long, long way, and finally reached the sea. There they built a boat and sailed across the sea to Ogre Island.

When they came within sight of the island, they could see that the ogres had a very strong fort there. And there were many, many ogres! Some of them were red, some were blue, and some were black.

First the pheasant flew over the walls of the fort and began to peck at the ogres' heads. The ogres tried to hit the pheasant with their clubs, but he was very quick and dodged their blows. While the ogres weren't looking, the monkey slipped into the fort and opened the gate. Then Momotaro and the brown dog rushed into the fort.

It was a terrible battle! The pheasant pecked at the heads of the wicked ogres, the monkey clawed at them with his nails, the brown dog bit them with his teeth, and Momotaro cut them with his sword.

At last the ogres were completely defeated. They bowed down before Momotaro and promised never to do wicked things again. Then they brought Momotaro all the treasure that they had stolen.

It was the most wonderful treasure you can imagine. There was gold and silver and many precious jewels. Momotaro and his three friends carried all of this back in their boat. Then they put the treasure in a cart and traveled throughout the land, returning to people all the treasure that the ogres had stolen.

Finally Momotaro returned to his own home. How happy his father and mother were to see him! They were very rich now with the remaining treasure that Momotaro had brought back, and they all lived together very, very happily.

The Magic Teakettle

There was once an old priest who was very fond of drinking tea. He always made the tea himself and was very fussy about the utensils he used. One day in an old secondhand shop he discovered a beautiful iron kettle used for boiling water for tea. It was a very old and rusty kettle, but the old priest could see its beauty beneath the rust. So he bought it and took it back to his temple. He polished the kettle until all the rust was gone, and then he called together his two young pupils, who lived with him in the temple.

"Just look at what a fine kettle I bought today," he said to them. "Now I'll boil some water with it and make us all some delicious tea."

So he put the kettle over a charcoal fire, and they all sat around waiting for the water to boil. The kettle started getting hotter and hotter, and then suddenly a very strange thing happened—the kettle grew the head of a badger, and a bushy badger tail, and four little badger feet!

"Ouch! It's hot!" cried the kettle. "I'm burning, I'm burning!" And with these words the kettle jumped off the fire and began running around the room on its badger feet.

The old priest was very surprised, but he didn't want to lose his kettle. "Quick! Quick!" he said to his two pupils, "Don't let it get away! Catch it!"

One pupil grabbed a broom and the other a pair of fire tongs. And away the two of them went, chasing after the kettle. When they finally caught it, the badger head and the bushy badger tail and the four little badger feet disappeared, and it became an ordinary kettle again.

"This is most strange," said the old priest. "This must be a bewitched teakettle! Now, we don't want anything like this around the temple. We must get rid of it."

Just then a junk dealer came by the temple. The old priest took the teakettle out to him and said, "Here's an old iron kettle I'd like to sell, Mr. Junkman. Just give me whatever you think it's worth."

The junk dealer weighed the kettle with his scale and then bought it from the old priest for a very low price. He went home whistling, pleased at having found such a bargain.

That night the junk dealer went to sleep and all the house was very quiet. Suddenly a voice called out, "Mr. Junkman! Oh, Mr. Junkman!"

The junk dealer opened his eyes. "Who's that calling me?" he said, lighting a lamp.

And there he saw the kettle, standing by his pillow, with a badger's head, and a bushy badger tail, and four little badger feet. The junk dealer said with surprise, "Aren't you the kettle I bought from the old priest today?"

"Yes, it's me," said the kettle. "But I'm not an ordinary kettle. I'm really a badger in disguise and my name is Bumbuku, which means 'good luck.' That old priest put me over a fire and burned me, so I ran away from him. But if you treat me kindly and feed me well and never put me over a fire, I'll stay with you and help you make your fortune."

"Why, this is very strange," said the junk dealer. "How can you help me make my fortune?"

"I can do all sorts of wonderful tricks," said the kettle, waving his bushy badger tail. "All you have to do is to put me in a show and sell tickets to the people who will come to see me perform."

The junk dealer thought this was a splendid idea. The very next day he built a little theater in his yard and put up a sign that said, "Bumbuku, The Magic Teakettle of Good Luck, and His Extraordinary Tricks!"

Every day more and more people came to see Bumbuku. The junk dealer would sell tickets and when the theater was full he would go inside and start beating a big drum. Bumbuku would come out and dance and

do all sorts of acrobatics. The trick that pleased people most was when Bumbuku walked across a tightrope carrying a paper parasol in one hand and a fan in the other. People found this most wonderful and would cheer and cheer for Bumbuku. And after every show the junk dealer would give Bumbuku delicious rice cakes to eat.

The junk dealer sold so many tickets that he finally became a rich man. One day he said to Bumbuku, "You must be very tired of doing these tricks every day. I have all the money I need. Why don't I take you back to the temple, where you will be able to live quietly?"

"Well," said Bumbuku, "I am getting a little tired and wouldn't mind spending my time quietly in a temple. But that old priest might put me on the fire again, and he might never give me delicious rice cakes."

"Just leave everything to me," said the junk dealer.

The next morning, the junk dealer took Bumbuku back to the temple. There he explained to the old priest everything that had happened and told him about the good fortune that Bumbuku had brought. When he had finished, the junk dealer asked, "So will you please let Bumbuku live here quietly, always feeding him rice cakes and never putting him over the fire?"

"Indeed I will," said the old priest. "He shall have the place of honor in our treasure house. Bumbuku is truly a magic kettle of good luck, and I'd never have put him over the fire if I'd known!"

So the old priest called for his two pupils and together they placed Bumbuku on a wooden stand. Then they carried Bumbuku to the temple treasure house and placed some rice cakes beside him.

It is said that Bumbuku is still there in the treasure house of the temple today, where he is very happy. He is given delicious rice cakes to eat every day, and never, ever put over a fire. He is peaceful and happy.

Monkey-Dance and Sparrow-Dance

Once there was an old woodcutter who went so far into the mountains one day for firewood that he became lost. He walked for a long time, not knowing where he was going, until he suddenly heard music in the distance and smelled the wonderful aroma of food and drink.

Climbing to the top of a hill, the old woodcutter saw a great crowd of monkeys. They were eating and dancing and singing, and drinking a wine that they had made from rice. The wine smelled so good that the old woodcutter wanted some for himself.

The monkeys sang and danced beautifully, much to the old woodcutter's surprise. Then one of the monkeys filled a gourd with wine and told the other monkeys that it was time for him to go home. The other monkeys wished him farewell. The old woodcutter decided to follow the monkey to see if he could get some of the wine for himself.

Before long, the wine gourd grew too heavy for the monkey to carry. He stopped and poured some of the wine into a small jar. He put the jar on his head, balancing it carefully, then hid the gourd in the hollow of an old tree and went merrily on his way.

The old woodcutter had been watching all this from behind a tree. When the monkey was gone, he said to himself, "Surely the monkey won't mind if I just borrowed some of his wine." So he ran to the hollow tree and filled his own gourd with some of the wine. "This is wonderful," he thought. "If this wine tastes as good as it smells, it must be very fine indeed! I'll give this to my wife—*if* I can find my way home."

While the old woodcutter was lost in the mountains, his wife was having her own adventure. She was washing clothes under a tree when she noticed the sparrows above her having a party. They were drinking a wine that smelled so good the old woman just had to have some.

So, when the sparrows had finished dancing and singing, the old woman quickly tucked one of their wine gourds under her robe and hurried home. "I'll give this to my husband," she thought, "and if it tastes as good as it smells, it must be very fine indeed!"

No sooner had she arrived home than her husband also appeared, having finally found his way. "I have something for you!" they said at the same time. They told each other their amazing stories, then exchanged their wine gourds and drank deeply.

The wine tasted delicious. But no sooner had they drunk it than they both felt an uncontrollable desire to dance and sing. The old woman began to chatter and jump around like a monkey, while the old woodcutter held out his arms and chirped like a sparrow.

First the old woodcutter sang:

"One hundred sparrows dance in the spring,

Chirp-a chirp, chirp-a chirp, ching!"

Then the old woman sang:

"One hundred monkeys making a clatter,

Chatter-chat, chatter-chat, chatter!"

They made so much noise that their landlord came running to their house. There he saw the old woman dancing like a monkey, and the old woodcutter dancing like a sparrow.

"Here, here!" said the landlord. "This will never do! A woman's dance should be graceful and ladylike, like a sparrow's, and a man's dance should be bold and manly, like a monkey's! Not the other way round!"

When the old couple finally stopped dancing, they told the landlord their adventures. "Well, of course!" He said. "You've been drinking the wrong wine. Why don't you exchange gourds and see what happens."

After that the old woodcutter always drank the monkey wine, and danced in a very manly way. And the old woman always drank the sparrow wine, and danced in a very ladylike way. Everyone who saw them dance thought them very lovely and started imitating them. And that is why to this day men leap about nimbly and boldly when they dance, while women are much more graceful and birdlike when they dance.

The Long-Nosed Goblins

Long ago there were two long-nosed goblins who lived in the high mountains of northern Japan. One was a green goblin and the other a red goblin. They were both very proud of their noses, which they could extend for many, many leagues across the land, and they were always arguing as to who had the most beautiful nose.

One day the green goblin was resting on top of his mountain when he smelled something very good coming from somewhere down on the plains. "My, but something smells good," he said. "I wonder what it is!"

So he started extending his nose, making it grow longer and longer as it followed the smell. His nose grew so long that it crossed seven mountains, went down into the plains, and finally ended up at a great lord's mansion.

Inside the mansion, the lord's young daughter, Princess White Flower, was having a party. Many princesses had come to the party, and Princess White Flower was showing them her rare and beautiful robes. They had opened the treasure house and taken out the wonderful clothes, all packed in incense. It was the incense that the green goblin had smelled.

Princess White Flower was looking for a place to hang her robes so that everyone could see them better. When she caught sight of the green goblin's nose, she said, "Oh, look, someone's hung a green pole here. We'll hang the robes on it!"

So the princess called her maids and they hung the beautiful robes on the goblin's nose. The green goblin, sitting far away on his mountain, felt something tickling his nose, so he began pulling it back in.

When the princesses saw the beautiful robes flying away through the air, they were very surprised. They tried to take back the robes, but they were too late.

The green goblin was very pleased when he saw the beautiful robes hanging from his nose. He gathered them up and took them home with him. Then he invited the red goblin, who lived on the next mountain, to come and see him.

"Just look what a wonderful nose I have," he said to the red goblin. "It's brought me all these wonderful robes!"

The red goblin was jealous when he saw the robes. He would have turned green with envy except that red goblins can't turn green.

"I'll show you whose nose is the best," the red goblin said. "Just you wait and I'll show you."

And so the red goblin sat on top of his mountain every day, rubbing his long red nose and sniffing the air. Many days passed and he still hadn't smelled anything good. He became very impatient and said, "Well, I won't wait any longer. I'll send my nose down to the plains anyway, and it's sure to find something good there."

So the red goblin started extending his nose, making it grow longer and longer, until it crossed seven mountains, went down into the plains, and finally ended up at the same lord's mansion.

At that moment the lord's young son, Prince Valorous, and his little friends were playing in the garden. When Prince Valorous caught sight of the red goblin's nose, he cried, "Look at this red pole that someone's put here. Let's use it as a swing!"

So the children tied some ropes to the red pole to make swings. Then how they played! They swung high up into the sky and climbed all over the red pole. One boy even cut his name into the pole with a knife.

How this hurt the red goblin, sitting back on his mountain! His nose was so heavy that he couldn't pull it back. But when his nose got cut, the red goblin shook the children off with all his might and pulled it back to his mountain as fast as he could.

The green goblin laughed and laughed at the sight. But the red goblin only sat stroking his nose and said, "This is what I get for being jealous. I'm never going to send my nose down into the plains again!"

The Rabbit in the Moon

Once the Old-Man-of-the-Moon looked down into a big forest on the earth. He saw a rabbit, a monkey and a fox living there together in the forest as very good friends.

"Now, I wonder which of them is the kindest," said the Old Man to himself. "I think I'll go down and see."

So he changed himself into an old beggar and came down from the moon to the forest where the three friends were.

"Please help me," he said to them. "I'm very, very hungry."

"Oh! What a poor old beggar!" said the three friends, and they went hurrying off to find some food for him.

The monkey found and brought the beggar a lot of fruit. And the fox caught a big fish for him to eat. But the rabbit just couldn't find anything at all to bring.

"Oh my! Oh my! What shall I do?" the rabbit cried. But just then he had an idea.

"Please, Mr. Monkey," the rabbit said, "gather some firewood for me. And please, Mr. Fox, make a big fire with the firewood."

They did as their friend had asked, and when the fire was burning brightly, the rabbit said to the beggar, "I don't have anything to give you. So I'll put myself in this fire, and when I'm cooked you can eat me."

The rabbit was just about to jump into the fire when the beggar suddenly changed himself back into the Old-Man-of-the-Moon.

"You're very kind, Mr. Rabbit," he said, "but you should never do anything to harm yourself! Since you're the kindest of all, I'll take you home to live with me."

And then the Old-Man-of-the-Moon took the rabbit in his arms and carried him up to the moon. So when you look at the moon when it is shining brightly, you can still see the rabbit there where the Old Man took him so long ago.

The Tongue-Cut Sparrow

There was once a kind old farmer who had a very mean wife with a terrible temper. They didn't have any children, so the old farmer kept a tiny sparrow. He took loving care of the little bird, and when he came home from work every day he would pet and talk to it until suppertime, and then feed it with food from his own bowl. He treated the sparrow as if it were his own child.

But the old woman wouldn't ever show any kindness to anyone or anything. She particularly disliked the sparrow and was always scolding her husband for keeping such a nuisance around the house. Her temper was particularly bad on wash days, because she hated hard work.

One day while the old farmer was working in the field, the old woman got ready to do the washing. She had made some starch and set it in a wooden bowl to cool. While her back was turned, the sparrow hopped onto the edge of the bowl and pecked at the starch. Just then the old woman turned around and saw what the sparrow was doing. She became so angry that she grabbed a pair of scissors—and cut the sparrow's tongue right off! Then she threw the sparrow into the sky, crying, "Now get away from here, you nasty little bird!" And the poor sparrow went flying away into the woods.

A little while later the old farmer came home and found his sparrow gone. He looked and looked for it but couldn't find it. Finally the old

woman told him what she had done. The old farmer was very sad, and the next morning he started out into the forest to look for the sparrow. As he walked he kept calling, "Where are you, little sparrow? Where are you, little sparrow?"

Suddenly the sparrow came flying up to the old farmer. It was dressed in the kimono of a beautiful woman, and it spoke with a human voice. "Hello, my dear master," said the sparrow. "You must be very tired, so please come to my house and rest."

When the old farmer heard the sparrow speaking, he knew it must be a fairy sparrow. He followed the sparrow and came to a beautiful house in the forest. The sparrow had many daughters, and they prepared a feast for the old farmer, giving him many wonderful things to eat and drink. Four of the daughters performed a beautiful Sparrow-Dance. They danced so gracefully that the old farmer clapped and sang along.

Before the old farmer knew it, the sun had begun to set. When he saw that it was getting dark, he said he had to hurry home because his wife would be worried about him. The sparrow asked him to stay longer, and he was having such a good time that he didn't want to leave. But still he said, "No, I really must go."

"Well, then," said the sparrow, "for all your kindness to me, l would like to give you a gift to take home with you."

The sparrow brought out two baskets, one very big and heavy and the other small and light. "Please choose one," the sparrow said. The old farmer gratefully chose the small basket and started for home.

When he arrived home, the old farmer told his wife everything that had happened. When they opened the basket, it was full of wonderful things—gold and silver, diamonds and rubies, coral and coins. There was enough in the basket to make them rich for the rest of their lives.

The old farmer was very grateful for the treasure, but the old woman became angry. "You fool!" she said. "Why didn't you choose the big basket? Then we would've had much more. I'm going to the sparrow's house to get the other basket!"

The old farmer begged her not to be greedy, saying that they already had enough. But the old woman was determined. She put on her straw sandals and started off.

When she reached the sparrow's house, the old woman spoke very sweetly to the sparrow. The sparrow invited her into the house and gave her some tea. When the old woman stood up to leave, the sparrow again brought out a big basket and a small basket and told the woman to choose one as a gift. The old woman grabbed the big basket. It was so heavy she could hardly lift it up, but still she carried it and started home.

As she walked along, the basket became heavier and heavier. The old woman began wondering what treasures she would find in it. Finally she sat down by the path to rest, and her curiosity got the better of her. She just had to open the basket!

When she did, all sorts of terrible things jumped out at her! There was a devil's head that made frightening noises, and a wasp that came flying at her with a long stinger, and snakes and toads and other slimy things! How frightened she was!

The old woman jumped up and ran as fast as she could all the way home. She told the old farmer what had happened, then said, "I promise never to be mean or greedy again!" And it seems she learned her lesson, because after that she became very kind and always helped the old farmer feed any birds that flew into their garden.

Silly Saburo

Long ago there was a boy who lived on a farm in Japan. His name was Saburo, but he always did such silly things that people called him Silly Saburo. He could only remember one thing at a time, and then would do that one thing, no matter how silly it was. Saburo's father and mother were very worried for him, but they hoped he would get smarter as he grew older, and they were always very patient with him.

One day Saburo's father said to him, "Saburo, I need your help in the fields today. Please go to the potato patch and dig up the potatoes.

After you've dug them up, spread them out carefully on the ground and leave them to dry in the sun."

"I understand, father," said Saburo. And he put his hoe over his shoulder and went out to the potato patch.

Saburo was busy digging up the potatoes when all of a sudden his hoe hit something buried in the earth. He dug deeper and found a big pot that had been buried there. When he looked inside it he found many gold coins. It was a great treasure that someone had buried long ago.

"Father says I must dig things up and then leave them to dry in the sun," Saburo said to himself. So he very carefully spread the gold coins on the ground. When he got home, Saburo told his mother and father, "I found a pot of gold coins and spread them out in the sun to dry."

Saburo's father and mother were very surprised to hear this. They ran back to the potato patch, but someone had already taken the coins.

There was not a single coin left. "The next time you find something like this," Saburo's father said to him, "you must wrap it up very carefully and bring it home. Now don't forget!"

"I understand, father," said Saburo.

The next day Saburo found a smelly cat in the field. He wrapped it up very carefully and brought it home with him, very proud of having remembered. But Saburo's father said to him, "Don't be so silly. The next time you find something like this, you must wash it in the river."

The next day Saburo dug up a huge tree stump. He thought very hard and remembered what his father had said about the smelly cat. So he took the stump and threw it with a great splash into the river.

Just then a neighbor was passing by and said, "You mustn't throw away valuable things like that! That stump would have made good firewood. You should have broken it up into pieces and taken it home."

"I understand," said Saburo, and started on his way home. Along the way he saw a teapot and teacup that somebody had left beside the road.

"Oh, here's something valuable!" said Saburo. So he took his hoe and broke the teapot and teacup into small pieces. Then he gathered up all the pieces and took them home with him.

"Hello, Mother," he said. "Look what I found and brought home." Then he showed his mother the broken pieces of the teapot and teacup.

"Oh, my!" said Saburo's mother. "That's the brand-new teapot and teacup I gave your father to take with his lunch today. And now you've completely ruined them!"

The next day Saburo's father and mother said to him, "Everything you do, you do wrongly. We'll go out into the fields and work today. Stay home and take care of the house." So they left Saburo alone at home.

"I really don't understand why people call me Silly Saburo," Saburo said to himself. "I do exactly what people tell me to do!"

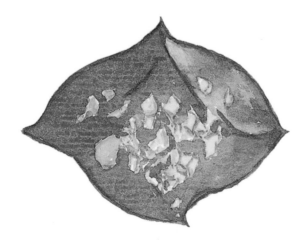

The Toothpick Warriors

Once upon a time there was a beautiful princess who had a very bad habit. Every night before she slept she would lie in bed and pick her teeth with a toothpick. That wasn't so bad, but after she was done, instead of throwing away the used toothpicks as she should have, she would stick them between the cracks of the straw mats where she slept. Now, this was not a very clean habit, and since the princess did this every night, the cracks of her straw mats were soon filled with dozens and dozens of used toothpicks.

One night the princess was suddenly awakened by the sound of fighting. She heard the voices of warriors and the sound of swords. Frightened, she sat up and lit the lamp beside her bed. She could hardly believe what she saw.

There, right beside her quilt, were many tiny warriors! Some were fighting, some were singing and some were dancing, but all of them were making a great deal of noise.

The princess thought that she was dreaming, so she pinched herself hard. But, no, she was wide awake, and the tiny warriors were still there! Though they didn't bother the princess, they made so much noise all night that she couldn't sleep at all, and when she finally did doze off, she suddenly woke up again because it was so quiet. It was morning and the tiny warriors were gone.

The princess was very afraid, but she was ashamed to tell the lord, her father, because he wouldn't have believed her. Yet when she went to bed the following night, the tiny warriors appeared again, and again the night after that.

In fact, the tiny warriors made so much noise every night that the princess couldn't get any sleep, and each day she became a little paler. Soon she became quite ill from not sleeping.

The princess' father kept asking her what the matter was, and finally she told him. At first he didn't believe her story, but he finally decided to see for himself. He told her to sleep in his room that night and he would stand watch in hers.

And so he did. But though he remained awake all night and watched and waited, the tiny warriors did not come.

While waiting, however, the princess' father noticed a toothpick on the straw mat. He picked it up and looked carefully at it, then called the princess to him the next morning.

He showed her one of the toothpicks. It was all cut up but the marks were so tiny that the princess could barely see them. She asked her father what the marks meant. Her father explained that the tiny warriors had come to her room because of all the used toothpicks! The warriors had no swords of their own and toothpicks made the best swords, and this was why they had come to the princess' room every night!

The warriors hadn't come last night, he said, because he had been there, and they were afraid. Then the princess' father looked at her sternly and asked why there were so many used toothpicks in her room.

The princess was very ashamed of her bad habit, and she admitted to her father that it was she who had stuck the toothpicks between the cracks in the straw mats, because she had been too lazy to throw them away. She also said she was very, very sorry and promised that she would never, ever be so lazy again.

Then she picked up all the toothpicks in her room, even those at the very bottom of the cracks, and threw them all away. That night the warriors did not come because there were no tiny swords for them, and they never came again.

Soon the princess felt better again because the warriors no longer kept her awake. She became very neat about everything, and pleased her father greatly by even sweeping the garden every day. She never forgot the tiny warriors, and if she ever used a toothpick again, you may be sure that she was very careful to throw it away properly.

The Sticky-Sticky Pine

Once there was a young woodcutter who lived in Japan. He was very poor but kind-hearted. Whenever he went to gather firewood, he would never tear off the living branches of a tree, but would instead gather the dead branches that had fallen on the ground. This was because the kind woodcutter knew what would happen if you tore a branch off a tree. The sap, which is like the blood of a tree, would drip and drip, as though the poor tree was bleeding. Since the woodcutter didn't want to hurt any trees, he never tore off any of their branches.

One day the woodcutter was walking beneath a tall pine tree looking for firewood when he heard a voice saying:

"Sticky, sticky is my sap,

For my tender twigs are snapped."

The woodcutter looked around, and sure enough, someone had broken three branches off the pine tree and its sap was running out.

Skillfully, the woodcutter mended the broken branches, saying:

"Now these tender twigs I'll wrap,

And in that way I'll stop the sap."

He tore pieces from his own clothes to make bandages. No sooner had he finished than many tiny gold and silver things fell from the tree. They were coins! The surprised woodcutter could not believe his eyes. He looked up at the pine tree and thanked it. Then he gathered up all the coins and took them home.

The kind woodcutter had so many gold and silver coins that he knew he was now a very rich man. Pine trees are a symbol of prosperity in Japan, and, sure enough, the grateful pine tree had repaid him for his kind act.

Just then a face appeared at the window of the woodcutter's house. It belonged to another woodcutter. But this woodcutter was neither nice nor kind. In fact, it was he who had torn off the three branches from the pine tree. When he saw the coins, he asked, "Where did you get all those coins? Look how nice and bright they are."

The kind woodcutter held up the coins for the other to see. They were oblong in shape, the way coins used to be in Japan, and he had five basketfuls. He told the mean woodcutter how he had got the coins.

"From that big pine tree?" asked the mean woodcutter.

"Yes, that was the one."

"Hmm," said the mean woodcutter and away he ran as fast as he could. He wanted some of the coins for himself.

The mean woodcutter came to the old pine tree, and the tree said: "Sticky, sticky, is my blood.

Touch me, you'll receive a flood."

"Oh, that's just what I want," said the mean woodcutter. "A flood of gold and silver!" He reached up and broke off another branch. The pine tree suddenly showered him. But it showered him with sticky, sticky sap—not gold and silver at all!

The mean woodcutter was covered with the sap. It got in his hair and on his arms and legs. It was so sticky, he couldn't move at all. Though he called for help, no one could hear him. He had to remain there for three days—one day for each branch that he had broken—until the sap became soft enough for him to drag himself home.

And, after that, he never broke another branch off a living tree.